Good Neighbors 2

Tales from the Barn

A TRILOGY + ONE = Four Tales

JOHN P. POREC

Illustrations by Pat Denney
More Inspirational and Epic Tales

AuthorHouse™
1663 Liberty Drive
Bloomington, IN 47403
www.authorhouse.com
Phone: 1 (800) 839-8640

Published by AuthorHouse 02/16/2019

ISBN: 978-1-5462-7788-0 (sc)
ISBN: 978-1-5462-7789-7 (e)

Special thanks to Barbara Fandrich for her usual excellence in editing and publication oversight.

This book, Good Neighbors 2: Tales from the Barn, *was written especially for Baby Leo Larson.*

Print information available on the last page.

This book is printed on acid-free paper.

authorHOUSE®

Wow! For you, _____.

These tales are written just for you,
our special friend and honorary neighbor.

Yours Truly,
Thomas Jefferson Crow

Hello there, Kiddos—I'm back. Thomas Jefferson Crow coming at you again from my beautiful neighborhood called Puget Sound Overlook and my street, Nisqually Drive.

I told you I'd be back as soon as I had something to "crow" about—and boy, do I! Once again you get my version of a TRILOGY. Remember, humans believe bad things happen in threes. So, to avoid "bad luck," I added one more tale. Humans!

Before I begin, I need to update you as to what's been happening. Dakota the basset hound is as spunky as ever, sticking her nose into everything and taking naps with Shelly the turtle. And, fortunately, Shelly hasn't been put on top of the fence post again.

Mello the kitty still thinks she has more than nine lives—but just in case, Ernesto and Ernesta the eagles keep an eye on her.

Floppy the bunny has kept in shape thanks to her constant companion, Bossie the Chihuahua (and Bossie still lives up to her name).

Finally, Alvin the blood hound and little Bessie live in each other's shadows. Bessie's dad smiles when buying Alvin his big dog bones.

So it's time to sit back and get all comfy again and be ready to be inspired by our old heroes and meet our new ones.

Yours truly,
Thomas Jefferson Crow

WELCOME TO THE FIRST
CHARIOT OF THE DOGS' PARADE!

TALES TO BE TOLD

Tale One
Meet Murry

A Story of Teamwork

Starring

Murry—The Therapy Dog
Chrissy—The New Little Girl
Missy—Alvin's Owner & Chrissy's New Friend
The Gang—Dakota the Basset Hound, Alvin the
Blood Hound, and Bossie the Chihuahua

And Me, Your Narrator—Thomas Jefferson Crow

A big hello from yours truly, Thomas Jefferson Crow, live from my rooftop perch on Nisqually Drive. And, Kiddos, I can't wait to share the first tale "Meet Murry" with you. But first, a little neighborhood history (make that gossip).

Our neighborhood has had a big house, which we all called "the Barn," sitting empty for years. Well, outta the clear blue, the "For Sale" sign had a "Sold" sticker on it. Gossip as to who bought the Barn was so thick in the air it affected my vision when flying.

The truth finally came out at a Neighborhood Association meeting. The buyer was not a big, traditional family but a group-home family! The Barn would now be home to kids with all kinds of disabilities and enough staff to take care of them. The best thing of all . . . every kid was allowed one pet. (Humans call these "therapy pets.") All my buddies, from my crow friends and family to Dakota the basset hound, Shelly the turtle, Bossie the Chihuahua, Floppy the lop-eared bunny, and Alvin the blood hound were thrilled. Some of the humans, not so much.

Some humans argued about everything from safety to privacy to property values. Other humans, as we learned from the first "Good Neighbors" book, can learn—and when they do it puts the humanity in our neighborhood. After a few too many meetings, humans earned our Good Neighbor status and welcomed our new and soon-to-be good neighbors.

For a while the walkers avoided the Barn or peeked from a block away. Dakota and her gang of Alvin and Bossie were more cautious than normal. But also more curious than normal.

Seeing all this, I had to bring in the most powerful crow in my family to protect the Barn. The day Abraham Lincoln Crow and his family arrived, I breathed a huge sigh of relief.

The first thing Abe told me he had to do was to get support from all of our local Mother Nature's pets and all the humans' pets. If pets are happy, the humans are happy. In other words, "A neighborhood divided against itself cannot stand," which is a play on an old family saying. Nature's and humans' pets would unite the neighborhood.

Then Abe and his family took the day off and went to explore the dump, so I kept an eye on the Barn from my rooftop perch. I saw two things happening. Dakota, Alvin, and Bossie were pacing back and forth on the sidewalk outside the Barn. They'd pace, pause, and wag their tails. But I knew what they were watching because I was too—the shiny-coated black dog. My favorite color.

I couldn't tell what kind of dog it was, probably a mix, and it looked and probably was powerful. His red vest sparkled in the sun. He was what humans call a therapy dog. The dog's attention was totally focused on a little girl next to him wearing thick glasses.

I watched as a lady from inside the Barn came out to get the little girl. I heard the lady call the little girl "Chrissy." She then told the muscular black beauty to step down. She called him Murry. But he didn't step down until he saw Chrissy safely inside.

Once safe, Murry went to the edge of the yard, wagged his tail, and from what I could tell invited Dakota, Alvin, and Bossie to visit. And boy, did they. A lot of sniffing . . . (dogs!) . . . but Dakota focused on the red vest.

I saw Bossie's human mom watching from her window. She wasn't a big fan of the Barn. Dakota's human mom came up to get Dakota. Smiling, she petted Murry. Missy, Alvin's favorite person in the world, ran into the yard and gave all the dogs a quick pat. When Missy saw Chrissy in the window, she waved like a little princess. Chrissy smiled and waved back.

I thought to myself, this is a good start. I can't wait to tell Abe.

Later that night I took my most recent addition, Theodore Roosevelt, T.R., for a flight lesson. We stopped at Bossie's home. I listened to what Bossie's human mom and her husband were talking about.

I learned the little girl, Chrissy, had a visual problem that was likely to get worse, probably the result of her diabetes. I told my little T.R. that diabetes was simply a problem with a human's body making the right sugars.

I then learned Murry was not only trained to help with her visual problem but was trained to detect when she was in trouble with her diabetes. Murry knew how to first help brace her fall, then get help.

Before T.R. and I took flight I heard the husband say, "And you were worried . . . it takes all kinds and this is a beautiful thing." T.R. and I agreed. Maybe we were winning her over.

The next day, things were the same. Chrissy playing. Murry watching. Dakota, Alvin, and Bossie now playing in the yard too. As soon as Chrissy went inside, Murry played with his new buddies. Oh, one more thing, Alvin's Missy asked to play with Chrissy.

All the neighbors were taking notice of what was going on at the Barn. More kids with all kinds of needs and pets began to play outside. Little Mello the kitty even started to hang around the Barn.

As time went by, Chrissy and Missy became inseparable. Which also means Missy and Alvin became friends. Although to Murry's credit, when he was in charge of protecting Chrissy he was in charge. Dakota, Alvin, and Bossie were behaving better at home.

The Barn was becoming the place to be. The early skeptics were changing their views. But that would soon be challenged.

One day when Chrissy and Missy were playing, they decided to go to the neighborhood park, a block away. As soon as Chrissy took her first step out of the yard, Murry began to bark to alert the staff. But no one came. Having little choice, Murry stayed by Chrissy's side as the two girls walked hand-in-hand to the park. Sensing something was wrong, Dakota, Alvin, and Bossie joined Murry.

They didn't even make it to the swing set before Chrissy began swaying back and forth. Missy squeezed her hand and tried to hold her up. Murry was positioning himself tightly next to her, and he turned to Dakota, Alvin, and Bossie and gave two quick, short barks.

Now, I don't speak any Dog but it was a good thing Dakota's gang did. Missy continued holding Chrissy's hand, lowering her to the ground. Murry braced himself as the girl leaned into him, and in effect he lowered her to the ground. Alvin leaned into Murry for more support. Dakota put herself between Chrissy's head and the ground . . . a Basset pillow. Bossie snuggled next to her neck and started licking her cheek. Missy still held Chrissy's hand.

Murry, with the situation under control, took off for the Barn.

In what seemed like seconds, the staff from the Barn was on site. And, within minutes, a groggy-looking Chrissy was sitting up and even holding what looked like candy. Next, on shaky legs, Chrissy was led back to the Barn. And I swear, Dakota, Alvin, and Bossie were shaking as well.

Now, humans have a saying: "All's well that ends well." Interesting, some of the skeptics were happy with the response. But others just said, "See."

Later that night while reviewing the story of the day with Abe, Dakota, Alvin, and Bossie returned. Dakota gave her patented howl and Murry ran from the house.

Now, humans shake hands to congratulate for a job well done. Dogs—and this is what gets me about dogs—they sniff. A shake of Abe's head told me he agreed. "I'm going home, Abe, it's been a long day."

"Before you go there, Thomas, isn't that Mello the kitty that the eagles saved that you told me about?"

"Sure is . . . But who's she with?"

"Another cat, I think."

"Oh, boy, I'm outta here."

"One more thing, Thomas. I was checking out the neighborhood. And over on that inlet there's this crazy looking tree . . . even scary looking. What's up with that?"

"I'll tell you tomorrow. I'm beat."

Tale Two

Paradise Lost and (Fingers Crossed) Paradise Found

A Story of Redemption

Starring

Hattie—The Little Girl with "Up" Syndrome
Paradise—Hattie's Therapy Cat
Mello—The Neighborhood Curious Cat
Gorgeous—Mello's Mother
Dakota's Gang—Alvin and Bossie (and Murry When Off-Duty)
Abe Lincoln Crow—The Barn's Crow

And Me, Your Narrator—Thomas Jefferson Crow

Hey there, girls and boys! Thomas Jefferson Crow back to tell you the next story from my Puget Sound Overlook neighborhood. But first, a little update from the last story.

Chrissy is doing great. No more reports of that human blood sugar problem. And Murry, when he works he works, but since Dakota, Alvin, and Bossie came into his life, when he plays he plays. The only tough news is that Chrissy's vision seems to be getting worse.

We ended the last tale with Mello and the new cat. They are attached at the hip. So far. Mello doesn't seem to set a good example.

Now, if you remember, Abe asked me about that scary tree over on the inlet in what the locals call "Twisted Tree Grove." But before I tell you about that grove and the strangest tree in that grove, let me tell you about another fascinating tree here in the great Pacific Northwest.

There is an island not more than ten miles from here (the way we crows fly) called Vashon Island. It is famous for its Strawberry Festival, and most recently it is famous for the humans because of a great children's book that tells the story of the "Bicycle in the Tree." We crows still argue about how the bicycle got in the tree, but you can read the book and decide for yourself. I leave you with this: mysterious things happen in trees. Crows know this more than humans. And that brings me again to the strange tree old Abe was worried about.

Because I'm the head crow of my Puget Sound Overlook neighborhood, I hear all kinds of stories. But after years of listening more to crows than humans (they tell whoppers) I settled on this reporting.

First, this tree is the only cedar in the grove and it stands twenty feet higher than the rest of the trees. This is probably why the lightning bolt hit the tree and split it in half . . . right down the middle. But for some strange reason, the tree didn't die. In fact, it is still growing today. However, the tree was left with burned scars on the trunk—and this is where the hoopla starts. Rumors fly from "if you look at the scars you'll go blind" to "the scars are the faces of two hikers near the tree when it was struck." Those who brave looking at the tree swear the burned faces stare at you with the eyes burning like red coals. We crows aren't superstitious but none of us ever lands on that tree when flying by.

The other rumor that surrounds this tree is that there are diamonds created by the lightning strike buried in the roots. Although there are a lot of holes dug at the base of the tree, there've been no reports of diamonds ever found.

In a couple of pages you'll know why I told you about this tree. But now, back to our story of Paradise lost.

If you remember, all the kids who live in the Barn have pets. The pets are called by humans "service" or "therapy" pets. After seeing Murry save Chrissy in the first story, I know you'll agree these pets are special.

So while we're on the special topic let me tell you about Hattie. She is a little girl, twelve years old, and she has something the humans call "Down syndrome." But after watching Hattie play with her pet cat, Paradise, you would agree humans once again got it wrong. Abe and I think she has "Up syndrome." She's a little different, but in a good way.

What I've learned about Hattie is that she has a favorite place to go that she calls Paradise, and she has a cat that she named Paradise after her favorite place.

Paradise is a black and white female cat with brown patches on her back. Her color pattern often makes it difficult to spot her in the yard when she's playing near bushes. She's a bundle of energy and even gives Mello a run for her money. (You may remember Mello from the first "Good Neighbors" book . . . she was rescued by the eagles after she climbed on the roof.)

When Paradise isn't with Hattie, I often spot her exploring the neighborhood with Mello. And, to be honest, from my view Paradise often is leading the way.

One day, Little Hattie's cry could be heard throughout the neighborhood. I flew over to the Barn to see Abe and check things out. Paradise was missing. We watched as some staff tried to calm Hattie down while others were organizing a search party.

Murry let out a couple of loud barks, and out of nowhere came Dakota, Alvin, and Bossie. Right behind them was Mello, without Paradise but with her mother, Gorgeous. Now, neither Abe nor I speak Cat, but we could tell that Mello was getting the third degree from her mother. Soon everyone was giving Mello the third degree. I'm no detective but from my viewpoint, Mello didn't know anything.

Next I saw a human, Hattie's teacher, with a blanket. She called Murry over for a sniff. Murry was a great dog but when it came to smelling he needed Dakota and Alvin. With one bark, Dakota, Alvin, and Bossie came to the edge of the yard. One more bark and the gang broke the rule and ran to the blanket. Before I could say their names they huddled and were off on the scent, Mello in hot pursuit.

Hattie took off too but was quickly stopped by the staff telling her everything would be fine. She wasn't buying it.

Abe and I were providing support from the air while following Dakota and the gang. It didn't take us long to know where we were heading . . . Twisted Tree Grove! And if we needed more proof, Mello split from the dogs and took a shortcut to "the tree." Soon everyone was there. Abe and I watched from the next tree over.

The staff was calling for Paradise while Dakota and Alvin's noses were working the old diamond holes. Half of Dakota was down one hole, Alvin was too big to fit, and Bossie paced around and around the tree.

Now, a few pages back I told you how Mello had to be rescued off the roof by the eagles. But what I didn't tell you was that after that day Mello never climbed more than three feet off the ground.

Everyone watched as Mello ran and jumped, using Alvin's tall back as a springboard, and landed at least five feet up the tree trunk! And like the best gymnast you ever have seen, she scaled the tree using the branches like a trapeze. Her heroics drew a hush from the crowd. A tree branch snapped, causing everyone to jump. Then came a trademarked "meow," followed by another.

Dakota and Alvin howled, Bossie did a back flip, Gorgeous purred, and the staff clapped as Mello, leading the way and closely followed by Paradise, descended to earth.

Hattie and Paradise's reunion was one for the books. Abe nudged me as we watched the hugs and kisses.

"Well, Thomas," Abe said, nodding his head, "I learned two things today. First, I've never seen a cat, much less two cats, climb down a tree; usually they have to be rescued. Second, it was like what my namesake once said: 'Follow the truth wherever it leads.' Mello was innocent."

I knew right then that I had brought the perfect crow in for the Barn.

Tale Three
Little Crow Peep

A Story of Communication

Starring

Teddy Roosevelt (T.R.) Crow—Thomas Jefferson's Son
Milo—A Perfect Little Boy

And Me, Your Narrator—Thomas Jefferson Crow

Hey there, Kiddos, Thomas Jefferson Crow coming at you from my Puget Sound Overlook neighborhood in the great Pacific Northwest. I hope you're enjoying the tales so far. A little update: Chrissy and Missy are doing great; Missy and Alvin are still sweethearts; Dakota is still her human mom's favorite; Bossie is, well, still bossy; and Floppy the lop-eared bunny is still staying in shape. And because of all of my friends, the inspiration for stories keeps coming.

Today's tale hits closer to home. My little boy, Teddy Roosevelt (we call him T.R.) is, let's just say, testing my patience. The Missus and I never had a problem, in fact, he was almost too good. But lately he thinks rules are for someone else. Now, humans might be able to get away with that, but in the animal kingdom broken rules can have severe consequences.

The problem started when one day I saw him over at the Barn on the roof. And he was pecking away at the roof like a woodpecker! He would peck, then strut around like he's listening. He was doing this over and over again.

I thought about talking to Abe about it, but I didn't want to bother him. The Missus told me it was a just a phase. I told her phases don't last six months. She told me to be patient.

One day I watched him peck, pause, listen, and peck some more. I lost my cool, and I did a fly-by with a buzz. This brought him home, and I grounded him. And when a bird gets grounded that's for real.

A week later, I overheard the Missus and T.R. talking. That's when I found out what truly was happening. T.R.'s mother gave him permission to go to the Barn any time he wanted—and she told me to watch and learn, so that's what I did.

I learned there was a little boy named Milo living at the Barn. He has autism, which the Missus explained means he has a hard time talking, listening, looking you in the eyes, and even making friends. Then she told me to put two and two together, so that's what I set out to do.

I watched T.R. peck the roof, pause, and listen. He did this over and over again. I noticed he always pecked on the same spot on the roof, then he would pause—so I knew he was waiting for a response!

I checked a little further and talked to Abe. He told me two important things: One, T.R. was pecking right above Milo's room, and two, Milo was tapping back.

Now, from a human perspective I don't know how they define communication, but to me, a crow, both had a purpose for what they were doing. I didn't let on to T.R. that I knew what was going on. And even if I did, when it came to communicating, T.R. and I were still on a different page. Kids!!

One morning after checking out the neighborhood, making sure everything was okay, and it was, I went to my perch to see if T.R. was at the Barn. He was, but he was pacing in the yard. After about fifteen minutes of pacing, he'd fly to his spot on the roof and then peck, pause, and listen. He'd then fly back to the yard. He must have repeated all these steps fifty times. Finally he flew home, gave me a glance, then went to his mother.

Later that night I asked the Missus what was going on. Once again she told me to put two and two together. I asked her if T.R. was still mad at me. She said yes. I asked her if we would ever talk again and she said we would, once he proves his point.

Two plus two . . . his point of view . . . prove a point. Wow, kids are tough. But he did have my attention.

The next day after I checked out my neighbors I returned to my perch. I noticed things were different right away. More staff than usual were in the yard. Kids were playing with their pets. But everyone was on one side of the yard! On the other side, T.R. sat by himself. He just perched there with no pecking, pausing, or listening. I knew when Dakota's mom was mad at Dakota she'd stand there tapping her foot on the ground, and that was what T.R. was doing. Tapping and staring.

I wanted to fly down and comfort him, but I knew he needed to prove his point. And adding two plus two, I figured that's what he was doing. But it's hard watching your kid grow up.

Finally, T.R.'s head popped up to the opening of the Barn's front door. The little boy, Milo, who looked like he was about nine, was standing there. I watched as T.R. studied the little boy. Milo didn't look around but walked straight to T.R. and stopped about four feet away. T.R. tapped his beak onto the ground. Milo walked closer and sat cross-legged in front of T.R.

Milo started flapping his hands like he was trying to fly but couldn't. T.R. pecked the ground, and Milo sat still. Next Milo cupped his hands together and extended his arms. T.R. took up his offer. He slow-walked to the boy and jumped in the boy's hands.

Milo let out a squeal that scared me half to death, but not T.R. He didn't flinch. After a second, T.R. gently gave three quick pecks on Milo's hand. This time I was ready for the boy's squeal, but I still jumped a little.

For the next hour, squeals and pecks everywhere! One other thing that was everywhere—smiles on all the faces on the other side of the yard.

That night T.R. and I made up. Two plus two is four and point was proven. I learned that this was Milo's first attempt at communication with anyone other than himself.

Now, humans have this big idea that only they communicate. Well, take it from yours truly—no, take it from my son, T.R.—communication is a gift for every living, breathing form of life.

Until next time—Thomas Jefferson Crow.

Tale Four
Chariots of the Dogs

A Story of Determination

Starring

Big Joe—Little Boy in a Wheelchair
Pitzilla—The Paraplegic and Lovable Pit Bull
The Whole Neighborhood

And Me, Your Narrator—Thomas Jefferson Crow

Hello there, Kiddos—Thomas Jefferson Crow back to tell you the final tale for this Trilogy Plus One, or as many now are calling it, a Quadilogy. Of importance for this story is that our little star, "Big Joe," the quad of quadilogy, is for real.

Big Joe, as he is called, is anything but big when looking at body size. But when you look inside, like we crows can do, his heart is as big as a full moon. Big Joe has a condition called by humans "cerebral palsy," which is why his legs and arms don't do what he wants them to do. That's why the human doctors use the word "quadriplegic." That's why he has to sit in a chair with four wheels. And his brain works great because he can make the wheelchair go everywhere just by blowing into a tube.

As you all know by now, Big Joe lives at the Barn with all the other humans facing, bravely I might add, challenges. Now, I could peek through the windows and I saw that Big Joe was a terror, even doing wheelies inside the Barn. But every time he approached the ramp to take him outside he hit the brakes.

In the last story, if you remember, my son T.R. helped a little boy brave the outside. But now I watched the neighborhood gang of pets hang around hoping that Big Joe would come out. Dakota, Alvin, and Bossie joined with Murry wagging their tales (oops, tails) at the foot of the ramp, encouraging Big Joe to take the plunge. Wagging tails soon turned into dragging tails.

Now, I don't know how this happens in the human world but in the crows' world it seems like every time you take some time off, in my case going to the dump, something big always happens. And that's what greeted me when I flew home from the dump.

I saw something I had never seen before. And the reaction of Dakota, Alvin, and Bossie, with their moms in tow, matched my surprise. This was something not seen before in our neighborhood.

Standing, kinda, in the Barn's front yard, was one of the strangest looking dogs I've ever seen, attached to what looked like half of a wheelchair—a cart with two wheels, or something I've seen that humans call a "chariot."

In a nutshell, this strange dog's back legs were supported in this chariot thing. I had to do some research, which in crows' language means eavesdropping from roofs. My flock, led by Abe Lincoln Crow, was on a mission.

After two days of fact-finding let me tell you what I learned. First, the dog's name was "Pitzilla," and the staff called him "Li'l Pitzy." He was a breed known as pit bulls, which have a reputation among humans as scary dogs. For the record, humans made them scary. They weren't born that way.

To prove this point, Pitzilla was a paraplegic dog. Now remember, Big Joe was a quadriplegic, meaning his arms and legs didn't work. When you have paraplegia, this means half your body doesn't work. Poor Pitzilla had lost the use of his back legs. But what is even sadder, this loss came at the hands of humans.

Let me explain. Humans, bad humans, train this kind of dog, "pit bull," to fight. Yeah, that's right, what I just said. Bad humans used this kind of dog to make them happy by teaching them to fight. And fights make these humans happy. Believe me when I say this, I know my animal kingdom is based on survival of the strongest, but this isn't to make someone happy, this is how we survive. We know our rules.

Back to Pitzilla—and this is disgusting even to me, a guy that likes roadkill—Pitzilla lost the use of his back half, or legs, from a bite in a dogfight. The bite cut his spine in half.

Not all humans are knuckleheads, and Pitzilla was saved by humans who trained him not only to use this chariot but to help others as a service dog.

This now brings me to the last tale for this second book of Good Neighbors because we are learning about good neighbors. In past tales we learned of animals helping animals, humans helping animals, and the great "spirit" that helps us all.

I knew what was going to happen. First, Big Joe and Pitzilla became fast friends. They were inseparable inside—and now outside.

There is always fun in our neighborhood but two things really make this old crow happy. I love Halloween for our baby crows because of all the candy left behind due to missed targets and distracted kids. The second, my neighborhood's Easter Parade, challenges the greatest parade in the world (which is, for my Southern California relatives, the Rose Bowl Parade).

What have we all learned since I started telling these tales? I love both my animal and human neighbors. The world could learn from all of us. But I knew horseracing fans would be in awe from what happened on that special Saturday morning.

I'm a nosy crow but this parade caught even me off guard. The banner strung between two giant cedars read: "Welcome to the First Chariot of the Dogs' Parade."

Dakota, Alvin, and Bossie all pulled their red wagons with Shelly, Floppy, Missy, Mello, and Paradise aboard. Murry pulled Chrissy in a cart. My son, I'm proud to say, sat on the shoulder of Milo in an old shopping cart. My bird friends, with Ernesto and Ernesta leading the V formation, flew proudly overhead.

And like a good human Santa Claus Parade, the guests of honor, Big Joe and Pitzilla, brought up the rear. Big Joe in his wheelchair and Pitzilla proudly by his side pulling his "Chariot of the Dogs."

Kiddos . . . I'm sorry . . . I only have one word left: "Wow!"

Later that night I flew over to the Barn to catch up with Abe. We both felt proud of our neighborhood. But Abe reminded me that at first more than a few were nervous about the Barn. The neighborhood had been divided.

Now, all that's changed. Abe reflected on another famous Abe's words: A house divided cannot stand. "Nor," added Abe, "a neighborhood."

Final Note

To all my loyal readers, no matter what size, or as we now know, no matter what abilities . . . there is always a silver lining. Thank you for reading this second book of Good Neighbors. I know for children's books one should keep everything happy or perfect. My feeling though is that these stories from the Barn are even happier and more perfect.

To my readers, I know this book describes new challenges from both the animal kingdom and the human world. But I hope we have learned that people are different. The Barn is a perfect example of this. To me this clearly demonstrates the true spirit of how our world should work. Compassion and acceptance should lead the way.

So, now, don't be afraid of things that are different because at the end of the day we have far more in common. If you open your eyes, ears, and heart, you will find it.

Thank you for reading this book. And let's always keep all the Barns in the world in our hearts. Don't be afraid.

Sincerely,
Thomas Jefferson Crow

THE END

Final . . . Final Note

One Year Later

Hey, Kiddos—I think it's important to give you one last update on our stars from the Barn.

Chrissy, the little girl with that sugar and visual problem, is doing great. She has not had a single fainting episode. And, as important, her vision has not gotten any worse and she's even wearing some cool glasses. She and Missy ride the bus together to school.

Murry still helps Missy and plays with Dakota, Alvin, and Bossie every chance he gets.

Little Hattie and Paradise still live in each other's shadows except when Hattie goes to school. I see her sometimes wearing cheerleader clothes and carrying pom-poms. T.R. told me what pom-poms are.

Speaking of T.R., he now rides on Milo's shoulder, listening to Milo's improving communication skills.

And finally, from what I hear, Big Joe and Pitzilla are the stars at the school. Seems all the kids are jealous of their "chariots." I even heard that they are going to race in what humans call the "Special Olympics."

In closing, all of nature's pets, human pets, and yes, even the humans, are "special." Just like my readers.

Yours truly,
Thomas Jefferson Crow

THE END

(I really mean it this time.)

Printed in the United States
By Bookmasters